MW00851220

Ellie
and the
Elven King

A Medallion Press, Inc. Book/October 2003

Published by:

Medallion Press, Inc.®
225 Seabreeze Ave.
Palm Beach, FL 33480

Copyright © 2003 by Helen A. Rosburg

All rights reserved. No part of this book may be reproduced or transmitted in any form or by any electronic or mechanical means, including photocopying, recording or by any information storage and retrieval system, without the written permission of the publisher, except where permitted by law.

ISBN 0-9743639-0-1

Printed in the United States of America.

First Edition

Anamosa Library L.C.
600 E. First Street
Anamosa, IA 52205

Ellie
and
the
Elven
King

by:
Helen A. Rosburg

Illustrated by:
Fortin & Sanders

Dedication

I would like to thank, and dedicate this book, to the following people:

Rafael Memoli - Valdemar, the Elven King
A man as beautiful inside as out

Leslie Burbank - Royana
Gorgeous, gracious queen; precious friend

James Rosburg - Tiko
My beloved. My soul mate.

Leland Burbank - George Munson
My favorite handsome hero and all around great guy

Jerry Maurer - Mr. Dalworthy
The man who was there when I needed him

Connie Perry, Costume Designer
Huge talent; treasured fairy godmother

and
Ali DeGray - Elliana Munson
My inspiration and truest example of all that is good and right
and beautiful in this world.

Thank you all. I love you.

Helen A. Rosburg - a.k.a. Fara

List of Illustrations

v	Elliana	33	The Gift
vi	Valdemar	36	"Elliana knelt before her mount..."
vii	Tiko & Fara	39	Valdemar's Profile
viii	Royana	41	Elliana
ix	Fara	47	"Valdemar lay sleepless..."
x	Tiko	49	"He hadn't thought..."
xi	The Will	51	"Oh my..."
5	"She held the letter..."	57	"He drew up his knees..."
7	"Forest at Longview"	58	"She was the shadow and you the light..."
8	"The house expected her..."	61	"Valdemar kissed away Elliana's tears..."
11	"She felt them before she saw them..."	65	A Moment of Reflection
13	"They flitted and hovered..."	67	Serenity
17	The Elven King	68	The Union
19	Mystical Forest	71	"Hand in hand..."
21	The Woman in Green	74	"Triumphant stallion..."
23	Before the King	80	"She was cleansed..."
26	Through the Willow Curtain	82	New Life
28	The Doppelganger	84	"King me!"
31	The Lovely Gown		

Elliana

v

Valdemar
vi

Royana
viii

Ellie
and the
Elven
King

"What the bloody hell?!"

"Please lower your voice, Mr. Munson," the attorney said calmly. "There's no need to shout."

"I'll bloody well be the judge of that."

"George." Elliana Munson laid a hand softly on her husband's forearm. He shook it off.

"Don't 'George' me," he retorted. "Just tell me what in the bloody hell this means!"

"It means," the attorney said evenly, "just what it says. As I have explained to you, the land, the house and outbuildings, are held in trust. You will not be able to sell them in your lifetime."

"Then *break* the bloody trust!" George Munson's meaty fist pounded Mr. Dalworthy's desk. He smiled grimly when the small, gray-haired attorney winced. "You, I assume, made the damn trust. *You* can bloody break it."

"I'm afraid that's not an option, Mr. Munson. Your wife's sister meant for her to have the property. And so she has it. Irrevocably."

"And *I'm* supposed to pay for the upkeep of this...this...*horse breeding* farm?"

Mr. Dalworthy and Elliana Munson exchanged brief, furtive glances. If the statement was not so sadly ludicrous, the attorney would have laughed.

"Of course not, Mr. Munson," he managed to reply levelly. "As you are well aware, Elliana and Rhiannon's mother, Wilhemina Ballard, left both sisters quite well off. Miss Rhiannon, who remained unmarried," he said pointedly, "managed her estate very well. There is more than enough income for your wife to oversee and maintain the farm."

"Oh, that's just grand," George drawled sarcastically. "My wife is going to *oversee* a bloody horse farm. And I'm expected to move out there with her? I'm expected to trudge around in *horse* manure?"

"I doubt that's what will be expected of you," Mr. Dalworthy said crisply.

"I...I don't think I even need to manage it personally," Elliana put in timidly. "I wouldn't necessarily have to move out there...would I, Mr. Dalworthy?"

Mr. Dalworthy clasped his hands on the desk and cleared his throat. "Actually, Elliana, according to the terms of your sister's will, you *are* required to spend a certain amount of time on the property. While there is a competent farm manager, Rhiannon felt that your presence, on at least a part-time basis, would ensure the continued well-being of her beloved animals."

Elliana shot a sidelong glance at her red-faced husband. "I...I suppose it really is a good idea, George," she told him nervously. "I wouldn't be gone too long at a time, so you wouldn't have to accompany me if you didn't wish to."

"You're bloody right on *that* score," he shot back.

"Well, I...I guess you'll let us know what the next step is, Mr. Dalworthy?" Elliana queried in a small voice.

"Certainly, Elliana." The small man looked relieved. "I've already given your sister's bank their instructions, so it won't be long before the income will become available to you."

"Then that's...that's it?"

"Not quite." Mr. Dalworthy opened a drawer and withdrew two envelopes.

"The bulkier envelope contains the keys to Rhiannon's...now your...house. There are several, and they are all labeled. This second envelope," the attorney said, voice lowered sympathetically, "is a personal missive from your sister. She asked me to give it to you should this...this unfortunate...day arrive."

"Thank you," Elliana whispered, tears welling in her eyes. She accepted the envelopes and slipped them quickly into her purse.

A long silence ensued, broken only by the routine sounds of the busy London street outside the windows of the law office, and George Munson's angry, stertorious breathing. Elliana dabbed the corners of her eyes with a cotton hankie.

"Thank...thank you, Mr. Dalworthy."

"Yeah, thanks. Thanks for *nothing*," George added.

Elliana exchanged glances with Mr. Dalworthy as her husband stormed from the room. "I'm sorry about..."

The small man waved a hand dismissively and came around his desk. He patted his client's shoulder in a gesture of comfort. "It's not your fault, Elliana. Just go on with your life and try to be happy. It was your sister's greatest wish for you."

Elliana nodded mutely. Tears choked her throat. As they spilled down her cheeks, she hurried from the room.

* * *

Elliana heard the sound of her husband's voice on the drive back to their flat, but she did not listen to his words. She clutched her purse, and the precious letter it contained, to her breast and fought the terrible grief that threatened to overwhelm her. She could still scarcely believe her sister was gone. She pressed the damp handkerchief to her eyes once more.

The end had not been entirely unexpected. Her sister's health, always fragile, had deteriorated over the years. The last year and a half she had been confined to a wheelchair, and had been unable to ride her prized and beloved horses. Yet she had always seemed so, well, *happy*, Elliana thought to herself. Right up until the end she had seemed positively glowing. In a way it was a comfort, she had to admit. Rhiannon had passed quietly, a smile still on her lips.

Elliana's eyes were dry by the time George parked and exited the car, slamming the door loudly in his wake. He stormed into their building without even looking back to see if his wife followed. Elliana sighed, but remained where she was. This was, perhaps, the perfect moment to read her sister's letter.

There was a single sheet of paper inside the envelope. Elliana withdrew it, fingers trembling slightly, and began to read.

'My Dearest Ellie,

As you read this, I know your heart will be heavy. But be comforted, for I lived a full and joyful life. You might even say my life was filled with 'magic'.

My passing has been made easier by the knowledge that you will take on the responsibility of caring for my animals. I know I never actually discussed it with you. But we shared the dream of this farm as children, and I truly believe that the dream still lives in your heart.'

Elliana's vision blurred with tears. She held the letter briefly to her breast and swallowed the painful lump in her throat.

Yes. Rhiannon was right. She had always harbored the hope that she might some day work again with the animals she and her sister loved so deeply. If only George...

Elliana shook her head. She didn't want to think about her husband at the moment. She smoothed the letter out on her lap once again and resumed reading.

'I would ask one final favor of you, darling sister, and pray you will not fail me. The only difficulty I have had in leaving this life is knowing how terribly you will grieve. I would have you do something that I know will ease your pain. Do you remember what we did when Mother died?'

Without even realizing it, Elliana nodded. The ghost of a smile touched the corners of her mouth.

'Do the same thing again, Ellie. For me. Do it soon. The mares are in the south pasture.

Forever, your adoring sister,

Rhiannon'

Almost without thinking, Elliana pulled her own set of keys from her purse and slid over into the driver's seat. She backed out of the parking space and pulled out into traffic. At this time of day, she figured, she could be there in under four hours.

She didn't even look back.

*   *   *

Longview had been aptly named. Acre upon acre of green, gently rolling hills stretched before the eye. In the far distance Elliana saw the dark line of forest that swept away, beyond sight, into the horizon. She brought the car to a stop momentarily and took in the scene spread out before her. Near the perimeter of the farm was a cluster of buildings that included the main house, the manager's home, the stallion barn and foaling barn, and various service buildings. White-fenced paddocks dotted the grand landscape and dozens of horses grazed, heads down, tails swishing. Elliana put the car back into gear and pulled onto the long, winding drive.

"Miss Ellie." The manager greeted her when she pulled up to the sprawling stone and timber 'cottage' that had been her sister's home. "The missus and I are glad you've come. It was your sister's greatest wish."

"I'm glad, too, Tim," she replied as she stepped from the car. "And this visit is long overdue."

The tall, thin man twisted his hat in his fingers and bobbed his head. "You're here now. That's all as matters."

"Thank you, Tim."

"Is there anything I can do for you?"

Elliana shook her head. "I...I think I'd just like to be alone for awhile."

"As you like, Miss Ellie. I'll be in the barn if y'need me."

She smiled by way of reply. When Tim had disappeared into the long, low barn, she walked up the flagged path to the familiar front door.

The key was well used and slipped easily into the lock. Elliana turned it. The door creaked open, as if the house expected her. Awaited her. She stepped across the threshold.

The faint, lingering odor of Rhiannon's favorite pot pourri. The hall table with the Chinese vase. The wide entranceway to the large and homey living room with its overstuffed furniture, chintz covered. Fireplace with its carved mahogany mantle. Mullioned windows overlooking a typical English country garden. The familiarity of it all struck her to the core.

Tears crowded her throat again. Leaving her keys on the hall table, Elliana turned and fled the house. She was going to fulfill her sister's final request. Now.

'The mares are in the south pasture', Rhiannon had written. Elliana left the flagged path and went around the side of the house. She broke into a jog when she saw the paddock ahead. Her breath hitched and she choked on a sob.

The south pasture was the largest of all. Rhiannon's magnificent herd of pureblood Arab mares had long occupied the vast acreage, running nearly wild over the hills to the very edge of the dark, dense wood. Just as she had expected, the horses bolted and galloped away, tails streaming, when they caught sight of her climbing the fence. Nearly blinded by her tears, Elliana walked slowly toward the treeline.

It had been nearly fifteen years since their mother had passed away. They had been heartbroken, devastated. It was Rhiannon who had held them together, who had known exactly what to do for their terrible grief.

"Come on, Ellie," she had said. "Let's go see the mares. They'll know what to do. You know Mother always said they had healing spirits."

And so they had trekked out to the south pasture, climbed the fence and watched the noble animals bolt from them. Elliana had wanted to stop.

"No, Ellie. They'll come. You'll see."

They had walked almost to the other side of the paddock, into the shadow of the wood.

"Lie down with me, Ellie."

She hadn't hesitated. They had both been raised around horses, they both loved them and trusted their gentle natures. Elliana lay down at her sister's side, the green grass cool beneath her back.

She had felt them before she saw them. It was like that again. Elliana closed her eyes and felt the thunder of their hooves on the ground. Then she heard them, pounding, breath chuffing loudly. She opened her eyes.

They had surrounded her. They moved in slowly, heads down, small pointed ears pricked forward curiously. Elliana lay absolutely still. The mares halted.

The eldest of them was the leader, Arabaska, a gray mare turned nearly white now with age. She took a tentative step forward, then another. She nuzzled Elliana, blew her warm, grass fragrant breath over Elliana's cheek. The other mares advanced.

It was exactly as it had been so many years before. She felt the grief, the awful pain, begin to seep away. Whatever magic the spirits of the horses possessed, they shared it with her. Slowly, her tears dried. Her heart eased. She closed her eyes and drifted away on a cool, cottony cloud.

*   *   *

She was in the place of 'almost sleep', as they had called it when they were little. She continued to float, neither asleep nor fully awake, hazy and comfortable, content. When she first heard the sound it was so improbable, so odd and unlikely, that she wasn't actually certain she had heard it at all. Elliana continued to lay perfectly still, eyes closed.

Then she heard it again. A high, tinkling laugh. There was no doubt.

Another burst of laughter, still high, but in a slightly different octave. The voices mingled, trilled. Elliana opened her eyes.

She was dreaming. Surely she was asleep and dreaming.

They were tiny, no bigger than her little finger. Pale, gauzy wings sprouted from their backs. They flitted and hovered, slightly off to her right. Their wings beat so fast she could barely see them. But she could see what they were doing.

More laughter. The little male had the female's clothing off now. The minuscule pink buds of her breasts shivered in time to the buzzing of her wings. A grin on her saucy little face, she reached for the male's trousers and tugged. They came away and his miniature manhood was loosed. Fully erect, it pointed at the sky. He grabbed

"It is slight," Royana replied. "But it is there."

Valdemar briefly closed his eyes. He sighed heavily. "Very well," he said at length. "I will see her now."

* * *

Maybe it wasn't a dream, Elliana said to herself. Maybe, when she had laid down in the grassy pasture, she had inhaled the pollen of some rare hallucinogen. Yes, that was it. She was plain, old fashioned 'tripping'. It was the only way to explain what she experienced.

The forest had changed when she entered it. It was subtle at first. She was aware something was different. She just wasn't quite sure what it was, but the close crowding trees gave her a much different feeling than any wood she had been in previously. It was almost as if the trees *watched* her. Like silent sentinels, they regarded her passing, prepared to strike should she prove foe rather than friend. Elliana stared back at them from the corners of her eyes.

She was surprised, therefore, when the dense wood suddenly gave way. Warm sunlight poured on Elliana's shoulders. Damp, moldy leaves and fecund earth became a velvety carpet of grass. The stern and towering trees were at her back, while ahead stood what appeared to be a willow grove.

"We're almost there!" Fara exclaimed. "Come! Hurry!"

There was a tug on Elliana's wrists and she stumbled forward. Had this grove always been here, she wondered? Had her sister known about it?

There was no more time for thought. Fara and Tiko pulled her forward through the cascading branches of an immense and magnificent willow. When she saw what was on the other side, her breath caught in her throat.

"Oh...my..."

"Sssshhhh," Tiko warned.

The space in which Elliana found herself appeared to be a vast entrance hall, but like none she had ever seen. The sides were composed of the boles of silvery trees that arced up and over, so high she was unable to see the roof they formed somewhere far above her head. The carpet of grass in front of the willow grove continued in here, but it was strewn with tiny wildflowers in a rainbow of colors. More of the blossoms were entwined in liana-like vines that were wound about the silver-barked tree trunks. Most amazing of all, however, were the people. If people, indeed, they were.

Cloaked in robes of earthen and forest colors, they moved throughout the hall in groups, pairs, or singly. Although 'moved', Elliana thought, was not the proper word. They appeared almost to flow, or float across the ground. They were slim, elegant and graceful people, their eyes slightly almond-shaped. Both men and women wore their hair long and straight, and the colors were unusual; porcelain white, silver, a thin and pale shade of gold. And all about their heads tiny creatures like Tiko and Fara hovered and buzzed.

To Elliana's discomfiture, all eyes turned to her when she advanced into the 'room'. The low hum of conversation ceased. Heads turned in her direction.

"She is here! She is here!" Fara announced needlessly.

The crowd around them abruptly parted to make way for a distinguished looking woman clad all in green. Her hair was white and, although her pale complexion was unlined, she gave the impression of age. She made a simple gesture and Tiko and Fara drew Elliana forward once more.

Flushing from the tips of her toes to the roots of her hair, Elliana hurried along behind Tiko, Fara and the older woman, wishing a hole would open in the ground so she could drop into it. Instead, she was drawn through another curtain of willow branches.

The space beyond was even more wondrous than that behind. Elliana had only

a brief glimpse, however, before all her attention was riveted on the man in the center of the glorious space.

He sat on a throne of curving, twisted willow wood, festooned with flowers of myriad variety and scent. Shirtless, his skin was as smooth and unblemished as satin, his hair so black it shone with blue light. Green light sparkled from his eyes, a green as deep and mysterious as forest depths. His features were sharp and perfectly symmetrical. His hands were beautifully shaped, fingers long and thin. His gaze impaled her.

The stardust bonds evaporated. Tiko and Fara disappeared into the upper reaches of the enormous space over her head. The white-haired woman moved to stand by the side of the throne.

"My son," she said simply. "Valdemar, King of the Elvish People."

Valdemar nodded subtly. Elliana had the ridiculous and overwhelming urge to curtsy. She managed to contain it, and nodded in return.

"And you," Valdemar said in an unexpectedly musical voice, "are Elliana. Welcome to my court."

Elliana hadn't the faintest idea how to respond. The entire situation was simply beyond her comprehension. King of the Elvish people. Pixies, fairies, a forest castle and sentinel trees. What in the world was she supposed to say? Or did it even matter? Surely, this wasn't real, wasn't happening.

"Have you nothing to say?" Valdemar asked, as if he had read her thoughts.

Might as well play along, Elliana said to herself. If it was a dream, at least it was a pleasant one.

"I...I would like to know, if I may, why...why I'm here?"

The faintest of smiles touched Valdemar's lips. Elliana noticed it did not reach his eyes. Their expression, in fact, was deeply sad.

"I have had you brought here," Valdemar said, "To be my queen."

Something happened in Elliana's chest. She thought her heart might just have stopped. She forced herself to take a deep breath.

"To be your...your queen," she repeated.

Valdemar nodded.

"And who decided this, may I ask?"

"Yes, you may ask," Valdemar replied affably. "And the answer is...your sister. Rhiannon. She is the one who bid me take you as my queen."

*   *   *

The white-haired woman waved something under her nose. Its odor was pungent, sharp. Elliana tried to push it away, but the woman persisted. Elliana's senses quickly cleared, and she realized, to her horror, that she was lying on the ground. She coughed and sat up.

The older woman rose gracefully to her feet, and Elliana noticed she held a sprig of herb in her hand. It must be what she had smelled, she realized, the odor that had revived her. Which meant she had fainted. Elliana pressed her fingers to her temples as if it might aid in clearing her head.

Rhiannon. Valdemar had said Rhiannon had wanted her to be his queen.

"No." Elliana struggled to her feet. She saw that Valdemar now stood before his throne, hands on his slender hips. She noticed as well how beautifully built he was. His naked chest was smooth and, while not overly muscular, toned and shapely. His biceps, too, were well defined. Clad in skin-tight leggings, however, it was easy to see his thighs and calves were extremely well developed. Elliana tried to keep her eyes from the V of his crotch, as it was easy to see he was equally well developed in that area, too. Something peculiar began to happen in the pit of her stomach.

"You said 'no'," Valdemar reminded her. "'No' what?"

Elliana swallowed. Could one faint in a dream? "No, I don't believe what you said about my sister," she replied at length. "I don't believe you even knew her."

Royana glanced quickly at her son. His gaze remained fixed on Elliana.

"Not only did I know her, Elliana," Valdemar said slowly, "I loved her. She was both the queen of my people, and the queen of my heart. Her death has stolen away the light in my life. My grief has no end."

It was in that moment Elliana knew she was not dreaming. It was real, all of it. The trees, the castle, elves and fairies. The King. The knowledge was like a punch in the stomach.

The white-haired woman started forward.

"No, I'm...I'm all right," Elliana said quickly. She drew a deep breath. It was real. But insane.

"How...why...why would Rhiannon, my sister...I mean..."

"Take pity on the girl, my son," the white-haired woman said softly. "You need to explain many things. Perhaps it would best be done in more comfortable surroundings."

"You are absolutely right, Mother." Valdemar removed his hands from his hips. "I fear my grief has caused me to lose my manners."

Elliana watched Valdemar walk toward her and, unaccountably, her knees weakened. When he held out his hand to her, she took it without thinking.

His flesh was cool, his grip firm. It felt frighteningly natural.

"Come. I want to show you something."

Hand in hand they walked out through the willow curtain into the main hall. Once again, heads turned in Elliana's direction. This time, however, it was not she who was the center of attention, but Valdemar. No one made an overt sign of obeisance, yet every gaze was filled with love, respect, admiration. Elliana cast a sidelong look at the king.

He looked straight ahead, the same strange, sad half-smile on his lips. A sudden rush of empathy tingled through Elliana's entire body. Empathy and something more, something that caused her heart to squeeze with apprehension. She stopped in her tracks and turned to Valdemar.

"I...I'm so sorry. I loved my sister with all my heart. I miss her, too. But you can't really mean to...to keep me here."

Valdemar's perfectly arched black brows elevated ever so slightly. "But of course I do."

"Surely you know I'm married!"

"Your laws mean nothing to us here."

"But I...I have a life, things to do."

"They will be done," he replied simply.

"I'll be missed! People will wonder where I am."

"Yes," he agreed, "they certainly would. If they noticed you were missing. They will not."

Elliana opened her mouth, but nothing came out.

Valdemar turned to a group standing not far away. "Meera," he said. "Please come forward."

A lovely young woman moved to Valdemar's side. She was slender, her face somewhat elongated, eyes uptilted. Her hair was pale, sunlight yellow, her eyes brown.

"Are you ready, Meera?" the king inquired.

The young woman nodded. She turned to Elliana and gazed deeply into her eyes. Then she began to change.

Elliana wasn't sure what she was seeing at first. Meera's face appeared to become fluid. Its shape changed, became rounder. Her eyes rounded as well and turned a gray-green color. Her nose shortened and widened a fraction and a dusting of freckles appeared on her cheeks. Her body became softer, curvier, hips and bust more pronounced. Her light hair drew up into curling waves and turned from sunlight into flame.

Elliana's jaw nearly unhinged. "She's...she's me..."

Valdemar's smile widened. "Indeed. For all intents and purposes, she has become Elliana Munson. She will speak and act exactly as you would. Your life will run smoothly in your absence. Just as your sister's did."

"Rhiannon wasn't my...I mean...when I was with her was she..."

"No, you never met Rhiannon's doppelganger," Valdemar replied in a gentle voice. "She did not spend all her time in the forest with our people."

'Our people'. The words had a curious ring to them. They reminded Elliana acutely of her current situation.

"Listen to me, please, you can't do this to..."

"You will, of course, need something more appropriate to wear," Valdemar interrupted smoothly. He snapped his fingers.

Elliana immediately heard a distant buzzing. It coalesced, moments later, into a flight of fairies. A flight of fairies and...Elliana gasped.

"What...what are they carrying?"

"Something more appropriate to wear, as I said."

"But..."

Valdemar raised a finger to his lips. Elliana fell silent and simply watched, nearly overcome with a growing sense of wonder.

The first group of fairies carried a length of satiny green material with which they surrounded Elliana. The second group set to work on her clothes.

"Hey! That tickles!" She tried to brush away the tiny, buzzing bodies, but the fairies were persistent. Within moments her suit was stripped away. Elliana automatically crossed her arms over her breasts.

"No! No!" she heard a familiar voice scold. "We cannot dress you if you do that. Arms out! Arms out!"

Although it felt ridiculous to obey the horny hoverer, Elliana struck her arms out for Fara.

"Up! Up!"

Elliana raised her arms to the sky. A cool, slithery material, almost like running water, slid down over her body. She felt dozens of tiny fingers tying the lacings at her back. She looked down.

"Ooooh. My."

The shimmering red/gold material flashed in the sunlight like precious jewels. The fairies pulled away from her, as if of a single mind. Elliana, hands pressed to her cheeks, continued to stare down at the lovely gown in amazement.

Valdemar nodded slowly. "Perfect," he pronounced. "It becomes you." The half-smile became a little less sad. "There is only one thing missing. Fara!"

The tiny fairy darted forward to hover in front of the elven king. He signaled swiftly with his fingers, imparting a silent order. Fara clapped her miniscule hands as if with glee, and Elliana thought she saw a Lilliputian drop of moisture on the fairy's small, rosy cheek. She flitted away, Tiko at her heels.

"What...?"

Once again, Valdemar lifted a finger to his lips. "Patience," he counseled. "Look. Here they come already."

Tiko and Fara returned, holding something between them. When they drew closer, Elliana was able to see they carried a pendant; a chain from which depended the startlingly lifelike reproduction of a fairy. The wings were iridescent, the eyes miniature gems. Wings fluttering frantically, Tiko and Fara placed the necklace around Elliana's neck and fastened it. She touched it where it lay against her breast.

Valdemar's expression had grown serious again. There was a suspicious glitter in his eyes.

"My first gift to your sister," he said quietly. "She only wore it when she was here. It is yours now."

Elliana looked up at last. "Valdemar, I…I don't know what to…"

"Come," Valdemar interrupted. "As I said, there is something I want to show you."

It was all too fantastic. Unbelievable. Yet she had to believe. It *was* happening. Mute, Elliana let the king lead her from the hall.

*   *   *

A broad, undulating plain stretched before her eyes. More of the silver-barked trees studded an occasional hilltop. In the far distance Elliana saw the hills grew more numerous, and larger. She thought she saw a mist clouding the crown of the largest. She stood rooted to the ground and stared in wonder.

"This can't be real," she whispered. "I've ridden every acre of this farm with my sister. This isn't really here. I'm not seeing it."

"Oh, but you are."

Elliana shook her head. "It doesn't even look like England."

"Not England as it exists today, I grant you," Valdemar replied. "But as it was long, long ago."

"How?"

"Magic, of course."

"Of course," Elliana repeated dryly.

"Would you like to ride with me over to the hills?"

"Ride?"

Valdemar did not respond. He pursed his lips and made a high, thin whistling sound.

"It's a good thing you're a king. You're not very musically inclined."

Valdemar smiled, genuinely. His teeth, Elliana noted, were very white and even. She might even go so far as to say his smile was positively dazzling.

"Your sister told me you had a wonderful sense of humor," he said. "I thank you for making me laugh. I did not think I would ever do so again."

Elliana noticed she was a bit short of breath. "You're welcome," she murmured.

"Ah, here they come."

Elliana looked up. Blinked.

The horses were small, but powerfully built. Their necks were thick and arched, forelocks, manes and tails long and thick. Their color was...

Elliana blinked again. Were they black? No. "Are those horses...green?"

Valdemar smiled. "Very, very dark. But, yes. Green."

They wore no saddles or bridles. One of the two animals was slightly larger than the other. He galloped up to the king, snorted and pawed the ground. The other stopped a few feet short of Elliana. He bobbed his head up and down and let out a little whicker.

Elliana laughed. "What's he saying?"

"Why ask me?" Valdemar replied seriously. "You can hear what he's saying as clearly as I do."

Elliana started to protest, but abruptly changed her mind.   She looked over slowly at Valdemar. "What did Rhiannon tell you?" she asked suspiciously.

He returned her gaze steadily. "Quite a lot."

"It...it was girlish nonsense."

"Not at all. Obviously."

Elliana turned her gaze back to the horse. "He's glad to see me," she said in a small voice. "He misses my...my sister." Tears welled in her eyes.

"Yes," Valdemar said softly. "You see, it wasn't 'girlish nonsense' at all. You hear them. You always have. You taught Rhiannon how to listen."

"It...it began at the racetrack," Elliana murmured. "Rhiannon was twelve, I was ten. Our great aunt took us because our uncle owned the track. She gave us each two dollars, and said she would place our bets for us if we wished. I insisted we go to the paddock to look at the horses as they were being readied. I told my aunt which horse I thought would win."

"You didn't 'think'. You knew."

"I suppose I did. I...just *knew* what they knew."

"And by the fifth race, according to your sister, your aunt's friends were coming by and asking who Elliana liked in the sixth."

Elliana looked up at Valdemar. He was grinning. She smiled back. He laughed, and she laughed with him.

"There. That's the second time today you've made me smile. I believe you have more magic in you than you know."

Elliana sobered. "Magic," she whispered. "This really is all about magic, isn't it?"

"A special kind of magic, yes," Valdemar said. "Ride with me. I will try to explain."

Elliana knelt before her mount, and extended her cupped hands as if in supplication. The horse dipped his muzzle briefly into her palms, acknowledging and accepting her. Elliana rose and mounted.

*   *   *

The horses were guided by the merest thought. And their gaits were so smooth as to be almost unbelievable.

"Aside from their color, and their gaits," Elliana said after awhile, "do they have any other magical properties?"

"They do indeed. They are the very core of the matter. They are the reason my people exist. They are the reason this very land exists."

The distant cluster of hills drew nearer. The mist became more distinct. But Elliana's vision clouded as she was absorbed into Valdemar's tale.

"England, as I'm sure you will admit, is a country obsessed with its animals. Horses in particular. There's a very good reason for that." The king reached down and stroked his mount's neck.

"People have long thought elves a myth, if they thought about us at all," he continued. "A myth of forest creatures, woodland guardians. Well, we are not a myth. And we are not tree wardens." Valdemar chuckled briefly. "We are, rather, guardians of the spirits of horses. These animals," he touched his horse's neck once again, "embody those spirits. As we protect and maintain them, so are the lives of their counterparts protected and maintained. As long as we keep them alive and well, the love of the horse will flourish in this country."

Elliana stared at Valdemar. It was too fantastic. So fantastic it had to be true.

"My sister knew all this," she said wonderingly. "She knew and never said a word."

"She was unable to. It's a part of the magic that helps protect us, the elven people, and, therefore, the spirits of the horses."

"So, Rhiannon knew, she remembered the times when she was with you, but was simply unable to talk about it?"

Valdemar nodded, but his gaze was far away. "Rhiannon was an amazing woman. She balanced her life carefully. She tended to her horses, her life in the 'real' world, her family and friends. And was a queen in mine." The sad, half-smile returned. "We spent many hours riding together like this. Her love for, and understanding of, horses made for potent magic. The animals thrived. *I* thrived. Our only true sadness was that Rhiannon was not able to share this part of her life with you."

Elliana looked over at Valdemar's elegant profile. "Until now," she whispered.

The king returned her gaze. "Yes. Until now. And I will tell you why." He sighed heavily and continued. "You well know of your sister's fragile health. Even though she was invigorated when she was here with me and, in fact, did not even need the aid of her chair, the magic air of my world was not enough to save her. Nor was it able to cure her barrenness."

Elliana flushed, but Valdemar did not seem to notice. He went on.

"Elves and mortals have always intermingled. Elves and mortal women, I should say. For elven women cannot conceive. We should be called the 'half-elven', I suppose."

Elliana felt something uncomfortable begin to push against her heart. "Did you know my sister was...barren...when you took her for your queen?"

"Yes," Valdemar breathed. He briefly closed his eyes. "You must first understand about this land, and its enchantment." He opened his eyes and gazed at the mist-shrouded hills coming ever closer. "This area, as you know, is in a remote part of England. We chose it long ago for that very reason. The woodland is vast, and very dense. It provides a shield for us and the entrance to this place where we are now. The magic of the spirit horses carries us back to what used to be, to the land as it was before the forest covered it, so we have space to ride, to live in. But it can exist only as the forest exists.

"For many, many centuries we had nothing to fear. Then more and more of the countryside was taken and developed. The world started to close in on us. Inevitably, someone bought the land that included our wood. That person was your sister.

"Fearful, my people and I, both the elves and the fairies, watched Rhiannon, trying to learn what she might do. As I watched her, and grew to know what kind of person she was, I realized her connection to horses. I realized how very special she was. How perfect she would be as my queen, the mother of my children. I fell in love with her."

"Finally, one day, I had her brought to me, as you were. I professed my love for her. I told her the things I am telling you now."

"And she consented to be your queen? Just like that?"

Valdemar's eyes shifted away from Elliana's. A flush of color touched his flawless skin. "Your sister," he replied at last, "said we could not marry because she could not give me the child I desired. The child and heir my people needed. She told me our time would be short, and did not wish me to grieve too greatly. She begged me to let her go. But I could not."

A spark of anger flared in Elliana's breast. "You mean you kept her a prisoner?"

"I could not let her go. The magic would not let her go. The magic that protects this realm."

The horse beneath her halted at Elliana's silent command. "But...but you said Rhiannon went back and forth, that she balanced her life between you and the 'real' world."

"Yes. She was free to travel back and forth once..." Valdemar turned from Elliana to gaze into the distance. He cleared his throat. "Once a mortal falls in love with an elf, a new magic is created. It makes it impossible for the mortal to communicate in any way about our realm. Thus, it is safe for the mortal to return to their world. *Our* world, here, remains protected."

"But if...if Rhiannon fell in love with you, as she obviously did, and was free to leave you then, why didn't you let her go? Why did you take a barren queen?"

As soon as she asked, Elliana knew. Love. Deep, abiding love. Her heart broke, and if biting off her tongue could have taken back the words, she would gladly have done it.

"I'm so sorry," she murmured finally.

42

A funny feeling tickled the pit of Elliana's stomach. An unsettling thought pushed at the edges of her consciousness. She pushed back. Lay down and closed her eyes. Hummed a little tune. Gave up and got dressed.

She had to see Valdemar.

* * *

Valdemar lay sleepless. His heart ached. He stretched out his arm and caressed the spot where Rhiannon had once lain at his side. His hand balled into a fist. He squeezed his eyes tightly shut.

He hadn't thought it would be this hard. He had thought he was prepared. Rhiannon had always been frail. They had known her time was short. Too short.

It had once been a rare thing for an elf to cry. But as they had become increasingly more human, so had their emotions. The First Elves, in their wisdom, had planned it that way. The elven people had been created to guard the horse spirits, until mankind well and truly knew the value of the marvelous beasts; not only their domestic value, but their spirituality, their healing powers, their very special kind of magic. This charge placed upon the elves was not meant to last forever, nor therefore, the elven people.

Thus they became more and more human with each generation. Ultimately, they would become completely human. The magic would be lost. The last of the pure elves, the ones who had chosen elven mates and a childless existence, would fade away. Only the fairies would remain, hiding in their shrinking gardens, living as they were meant to, in an endless celebration of life.

Valdemar dashed the unwanted tears from his cheeks. They would have made Rhiannon sad. He had never wanted her to be sad. He had tried to make every single one of her days special, memorable, filled with love and joy. For her sake, he must not become a slave to his grief. It was not what she wanted. She had wanted him to have again what he had known with her. And she had wanted her sister to experience what she had known. But was it possible?

Elliana was not Rhiannon, not at all. Rhiannon had been soft, feminine, gentle, ladylike in every way. She had reminded him, in many ways, of his mother. Her complexion had been pale and flawless, her hair the fairest strawberry blonde, her figure slender and delicate. Elliana, on the other hand…

A flurry of iridescent wings appeared before Valdemar's eyes.

"She comes! She comes!" The fairy announced.

Valdemar did not have to ask who as he started to rise from his bed. He did not have enough time to pull on the sleeping robe he had earlier discarded before she burst through the willow branches into his chamber.

Elliana was never quite sure how she had found Valdemar's room. Some primal instinct guided her. She needed him. She found him. She just wasn't prepared for the *way* in which she found him.

Elliana stopped dead in her tracks. "Oh. My."

Valdemar couldn't help but follow her gaze. A smile curled the corners of his mouth.

She wasn't too solid on her elven lore. One thing she did recall, however, was that elves were supposedly slight of build. There was absolutely nothing 'slight' about the elven king.

Flames redder than her hair rushed to Elliana's cheeks. Her breath caught in her throat. Her knees threatened to buckle. But she could not tear her eyes from the magnificence of Valdemar's manhood.

"Oooooh. My."

Had she spoken? Was that the sound of her own voice?

Elliana was finally able to slam her eyes shut. She pressed her palms to the fire in her cheeks. She groaned aloud.

"I'm soooo sorry," she whispered.

Valdemar laughed, his mood suddenly as light as it had been dark moments before. "Sorry for what?" he teased.

Elliana's eyes were squeezed so tightly shut she was certain her face would never unwrinkle. "For...for your...I mean my, *my* naked...no, no, I mean entrance. My entrance. I should have knocked. But there's no door. A door. You need a door. If you're going to dress that way, I mean. A door. So I could...I could knock." Slowly, carefully, eyes still closed, hands pressed to her face, Elliana attempted to back from the chamber. "Of course, being king, you can...you can dress any way you...you want, and *not* have to have a...a door," she stammered, still backing up.

Valdemar threw back his head and roared. He laughed until tears of a different sort ran from his eyes, until he had to double over and grip his aching sides.

Elliana stopped moving. Her hands dropped to her sides and she opened her eyes. "Are you...are you laughing at me?" she asked in a small voice.

Valdemar gasped for breath. He was only able to nod.

"It wasn't *that* funny," Elliana said crisply, stung.

"Oh...oh, yes it was," Valdemar choked. He managed to straighten up.

Elliana closed her eyes just in time. A new wave of laughter washed over the elven king.

"Would you *please* put something on?" Elliana begged.

Valdemar reached for his robe and slipped it over his head. "You can open your eyes now."

"Swear?"

"Swear."

Elliana peeked with one eye. She opened the other. "Thank you," she said tartly.

"My pleasure."

"I'm *sure* it was."

Valdemar couldn't seem to wipe the smile off his face. "Yes, well, perhaps you'd like to tell me now the reason for this pre-dawn visit."

"Visit? Oh. Oh, right." Elliana suddenly couldn't remember why she had needed to see Valdemar so urgently. The sight of him, unclothed, had been completely disconcerting. She made an effort to gather her thoughts. Then it came to her.

"I...well, I..." Damn him anyway for making her feel so self conscious. Elliana crossed her arms over her breasts and took a deep breath. "I came to ask you a question. An important one."

"I'm all ears."

"Is that supposed to be an elf joke?"

"I...I don't know what you mean," Valdemar replied, fingering his perfectly normally shaped ear lobe.

"Never mind. I came to ask you why Rhiannon... Oh, never mind that either." Totally flustered now, Elliana turned on her heel and prepared to leave.

"Wait." Valdemar caught her arm and turned her back toward him. "Don't go. Not yet. Remember yesterday I wanted to show you something? But we never got that far. Let me show you now. Please."

He was so close Elliana could feel Valdemar's breath on her cheek. Her heart somersaulted in her breast. She nodded.

* * *

Anamosa Library L.C.
600 E. First Street
Anamosa, IA 52205

Elliana heard her mount clearly again. Although 'heard' wasn't exactly the right word. It was more a simple knowing. She *knew* once again he was glad to see her. She saw the place in his mind he was going to take her. She looked over at the elven king and smiled.

"Yes," he said. "It's very beautiful. And it's special for another reason as well. Shall we go?"

He didn't need to ask twice. They set off at once at a lope, the skirt of her elven riding costume billowing in the wind.

The farther they went over the grassy plain, the hillier the terrain became. Stands of the silver-barked trees became more dense. The distant, misty cluster of hills drew closer. Elliana thought she heard the sound of rushing, falling water.

They climbed the outer hills and wove through valleys between. The sound of the water grew louder. Moisture clung to Elliana's skin, and she realized they had entered the misty area. They ascended a last, rocky tor, turned a final corner and Elliana gasped.

"Oh, Valdemar..."

The hidden valley unfolded before her like elegant embroidery. On the opposite side stood a towering hill, a small mountain really. Rockfall cascaded down its near slope, studded here and there with weeping willows, and over the stones and boulders flowed the clearest, purest water Elliana had ever seen. Mist rose all around it, and floated over the surface of the pool formed at the mountain's foot.

Valdemar gestured wordlessly for her to go ahead, and Elliana let her mount pick his way down into the verdant bowl of the valley. The elven king halted at her side.

"Is this what you wanted to show me?" Elliana asked.

"Yes. And more." Valdemar dismounted and held out a hand to Elliana. She joined him on the ground and twined her fingers with his. Butterflies awoke in the pit of her stomach.

Hand in hand they walked around the small lake. Near the waterfall Valdemar, assisting Elliana, climbed a foothill. At its summit stood a grand old willow. Valdemar sank to the grassy carpet, his back just touching the trunk. Elliana sat beside him.

"Is...?"

Valdemar pressed a finger to his lips, then pointed below at the pool.

She didn't see anything immediately. Then, slowly, the shapes began to form.

"They are the Horses of the Mist," Valdemar whispered. "The Spirit Horses. The progenitors of the lesser guardian spirits like the ones you and I rode here today."

Elliana's eyes widened. Never had she seen anything so beautiful, so wondrous, so fantastic.

The mist whirled and spun into two gray-white horses, tall and heavily, powerfully built. Their shoulders and flanks were rounded and smoothly muscled. Long feathers of hair trailed from fetlock and pastern. Their thick necks were gracefully arched, and their long, wavy manes fell to their shoulders.

As Elliana watched, mouth open, the stallion reared and pawed at the sky. His shrill scream made her cover her ears. All four massive hooves on the ground again, he pranced around the mare. Occasionally he laid his ears back, bared his teeth and nipped at her rump. She flagged her tail at him. His head came up and his ears pricked forward. He wheeled and pranced around her in the opposite direction. Now Elliana was able to see the evidence of his arousal.

"And I thought *you* were impressive," she breathed.

Valdemar had difficulty swallowing his laughter. He laid a hand on the back of Elliana's neck. Her flesh was warm, her hair a satin curtain to hide his fingers.

The stallion bit at the mare again. He reared and attempted to mount her.

This time it was the mare who screamed. She spun and struck at him, front hooves flashing. Then she ducked her tail and began to dissolve back into the mist. The stallion followed. In moments, both horses were gone.

"What...what did I just see?" Elliana turned her awe-struck gaze on Valdemar.

The elven king sighed. "The Spirit Horses came to you to show you their need. Their desperate need."

"I...I don't understand."

"Of course you don't." Valdemar removed his hand from Elliana's shoulder. He drew up his knees and draped his arms over them. He looked down for a moment, then up at the sky.

"The fate of the elven kings," he began at length, "Is inextricably bound to the Spirit Horses. As they live, and prosper, and...procreate...so do the horses. Their get, as I said, are the lesser spirits that guard domestic horses. But there have been no new foals, because..."

Elliana understood at once. "Oh, Valdemar." She laid a hand on his forearm. "I'm so sorry. But I...I have to ask..."

"Yes, I loved her that much," he replied before she could finish. "I risked my very kingdom for love of your sister." He waited for the tears to come, but they did not. He felt curiously comfortable and at peace. He looked at the woman beside him.

Something from Valdemar's gaze flowed through her in a hot rush. She could no longer deny it. He was the most handsome man she had ever seen. His gentleness

was a balm. The love he had borne for her sister was a path that led straight into her soul.

Elliana would never know what made her do it. She touched his cheek. Drew him to her. Touched her lips to his.

Valdemar responded, pulse quickening. His lips moved against hers. Briefly. They drew apart.

Elliana opened her eyes. "Why?" she murmured. "Why did Rhiannon want me to be your queen?"

"I have asked myself that question so many times. Now I am beginning to understand." Abruptly, Valdemar rose to his feet. "Walk with me?"

Elliana nodded her silent assent. Once again he took her hand. They strolled downward, toward the pool, then around and away from it, out of the mist and into the sunlight. Valdemar stopped and turned to Elliana.

"Rhiannon was a gift," he began softly. "But not one I was meant to keep. She understood that. She helped me to understand. She *tried* to help me understand why she wished me to...to take you. But I did not wish to lose her, and did not wish to listen, to hear. I told myself she wanted you to take her place to insure the safety of the wood perhaps. Or because you might, indeed, be able to bear children. I did not heed what she knew in her heart and soul. I did not realize, until now, how very, very deeply she loved me after all."

Tears welled in Elliana's eyes. Her lip trembled. "What did she...what did she know?" she whispered.

"That she was the shadow," Valdemar replied simply. "And you the light."

Elliana's tears spilled over and tracked down her cheeks. She made no effort to wipe them away. Valdemar tipped up her chin with his forefinger.

"Rhiannon made me smile. You make me laugh. You are all that is good and beautiful in the world, sunlight and life. You make me want to live. And love again." Valdemar kissed away Elliana's tears. He lightly kissed her mouth. He looked into her eyes. "Rhiannon knew something else as well. She knew it would happen exactly like this, in an instant. A moment."

To her dying day, Elliana would never forget the moment. She felt the wings of Rhiannon's spirit touch her soul. She felt cleansed and new. Whole. For the first time in her life.

"Will you take me back now, Valdemar?"

"Yes."

"Will I...will I be able to leave?"

It was a long moment before Valdemar responded. He drew a long breath. "What do *you* think?" he asked at last.

"I think...no, I know...I will be able to leave. Because I will never be able to stay away."

Valdemar smiled gently. "Every moment you are gone will be an eternity."

"It won't be for long. There's just something I have to do."

Valdemar nodded silently. Side by side they returned to the horses.

* * *

It was so strange. How long had she spent in this enchanted forest? A day and a half? Yet it seemed a lifetime. It had become her home. It was where her heart resided. And would forever more.

The elves who filled the vast chamber had all discreetly turned away. Elliana

There had been a costume party, years ago. Rhiannon and Ellie had gone as 'hippies'. But not the raggedy sort. Rhiannon had had her outfit specially made. The bellbottoms and midriff cut shirt, tied at the waist, were of white silk, heavily overlaid with yellow lace and embroidered with yellow crystals. Best of all, it had been made before Rhiannon's health had begun to decline. It would fit Ellie perfectly. She took it off its hangers, and rifled in the dresser for underwear. From a jewelry box she took a string of pearls and a pair of pearl earrings. She went back into the bathroom, turned off the faucet, sprinkled in some bath oil, stripped and sank into the hot water. She closed her eyes.

She was going to be a bride, a real bride. The thought was delicious. Scrumptious. She was in love, and loved. The fantastical magic part of it, elves, fairies, an enchanted wood, was merely icing on the cake. The greatest magic of all was simply the love.

When the water cooled, Ellie got out of the tub and toweled dry. She brushed her hair until it crackled and dabbed perfume at her wrists and throat. She dressed.

She was ready.

*   *   *

The fairies awaited her in the paddock by the forest's perimeter. They were unusually quiet, however, almost solemn. Ellie climbed over the fence, unassisted, mindful of her clothing. She walked into the shadow of the wood.

The patient sentinel trees watched her silently. They felt different to her this time, watchful, but in a kindly way rather than wary. Ellie crossed the verdant carpet of grass and passed into the willow branches.

The 'hall' was crowded and eerily quiet. All eyes turned to her, but this time Elliana did not feel self conscious. Every elf looked at her with respect and...she wasn't quite sure what. She didn't ponder for long. Valdemar approached.

He was cloaked in blue, iridescent blue, the cloak made entirely of bird feathers. His tunic and leggings were of a similarly iridescent color, but made of some silky material. It clung to him in ways she dared not dwell on at the moment. If she did, she feared she might faint. Already the emotion filling her breast threatened to overwhelm her.

Valdemar's expression was serene. A half-smile rode his lips. His gem-like eyes glistened. His blue-black hair swept back from his broad, smooth brow, and lifted a little in the wind of his passage. In his arms he carried something reverently.

Ellie feared her knees were about to betray her. Love welled in her like a live thing, writhing and twisting around and through her limbs, coursing in her blood, singing in her soul. Her lips parted as if to receive his kiss. Her heart beat frantically when he came to a halt in front of her.

Valdemar's half-smile widened almost imperceptibly. He unfolded the thing he carried in his arms.

It was a cloak like his own, but woven of yellow feathers, lightly tipped with red. The result was flame-like. Stunning. Ellie caught her breath.

Valdemar pulle the cloak around her shoulders. Royana stepped forward and fastened the cloak at Ellie's throat with a golden brooch in the shape of a willow branch.

"Once this was the gift from *my* king," she murmured. "Now it is yours."

Valdemar moved to Ellie's side, so both now faced the gathered elves. He took her hand and gazed into her eyes.

"You are my sun to warm my days," he said in a clear, strong voice. "I am your moon to light your nights. I am your king. You are my queen."

The crowd gathered in the hall made a sound like a collective sigh. Valdemar leaned down and lightly touched Ellie's lips.

"We are one," he whispered. "It's done."

The crowd parted and Ellie and the king moved through them. Hand in hand, heart and heart, they left the hall.

* * *

Ellie did not need to ask where they were going. Outside the umbrella of the great tree, the horses awaited. Their gleaming, dark coats shone in the sun. Ellie felt their joy at seeing her. Both animals nodded their heads in her direction, full, thick manes falling forward and brushing the ground.

Ellie approached her horse, prepared to mount. But he did something strange. He lowered his head again, bent his knees, and bowed before her. She stepped over his back and he rose. Valdemar mounted his own horse.

They rode in silence, side by side, over the grassy plain. The misty mountain drew closer. Eventually, Ellie allowed herself to glance at her king.

He had been watching her all along, she realized, smiling at her. Warm honey flowed through her veins. The corners of her lips twitched. She grinned at him.

"This is really happening, isn't it?" Ellie asked. "I'm not dreaming."

"If you are, we're sharing the same dream."

Ellie took a deep breath and let it out in a sigh. She returned her attention to the misty mountain.

Did the Spirit Horses know? Did they await them?

Something stronger than honey warmed Ellie's blood. She tossed her head and the wind lifted her hair. She raised her face to the sun and closed her eyes. Her feathered cape flowed away behind her.

Her life had been at a dead end. Now the world stretched before her. And not just any world, a magic world. A universe of love. All because of the man who rode at her side.

The emotion in Ellie's breast threatened to burst. Was it really possible she had lived all these years without ever truly knowing what love was?

Valdemar threw back his head and grimaced. He pulsed against her, longing for her, needing her more than anything he had ever desired in his life. He, too, felt the mist's caress, goading him.

Then, abruptly, the whorls and eddies of damp were pulled away. The air became electric. The ground shook with hoofbeats.

Valdemar plunged into Ellie with all the force of his passion unleashed. She cried out and he silenced her with his lips. She bucked beneath him, and he rode her. Her fingers clawed his back, trying to draw him closer, tighter. A low moan rumbled in her throat. Hot, slick and smooth they moved together in the eternal dance. Their bodies exulted. The wings of their souls united.

Off in the mist, the triumphant stallion screamed.

* * *

The days passed in a haze of pleasure. Ellie and Valdemar never left the hidden valley. Food and meadow wine were brought to them by elves they occasionally heard but never saw. Garments were left for them. They were never unfolded.

Like children, Ellie and Valdemar laughed and played. They rose with the sun, emerging from the folds of their cloaks, disentangling their limbs. They swam in the misty pool and made love in the warm shallows. They chased each other like colts in a meadow, and lay down to rest in the emerald grass. They explored the hills and found places to make love even Valdemar had not discovered before.

From time to time, they glimpsed the Spirit Horses. There would be a swirl of mist, a bit of breeze, and the mare and stallion would appear. Joyous, they pranced and nipped at one another. Eventually, he would mount his mate, trumpeting his desire.

The earth shook and sunlight glinted through mist. The world had never been so splendid.

But it could not last.

Ellie lay in Valdemar's arms. The sun sent out salmon streamers as it met the horizon, and a brisk breeze stirred. Ellie shivered and Valdemar pulled the fold of his cloak around her.

"Are you warm enough?"

She did not answer him. She did not, in fact, really hear him. Her thoughts were far away.

"I suppose...I suppose Meera must be getting anxious to return here for awhile," she said at length.

"She lives to serve in this manner. She will remain where she is as long as it is required."

"And I must go where I am required," Ellie murmured.

"It is time. I know." Valdemar leaned down and kissed her naked shoulder. "The horses will come in the morning."

"I'm not sure I can bear to leave you, Valdemar," Ellie said in a small voice.

"We bear the parting equally, my love."

Ellie nodded almost imperceptibly. "I have to go to London to...to take care of business."

"Yes. I know."

"I'll only be gone a day or two."

"There are, as you will learn, duties I must perform as well," Valdemar replied. "I will use the time to advantage."

"And be right here when I return?"

Valdemar smiled. "What do you think?"

"I think you are the king, and can do anything you please."

"I am indeed. And what I think I'm going to 'do', right now, is the queen..."

*   *   *

The sun had been shining when she left the forest, Valdemar's parting kiss still moist on her lips. Now, however, clouds gathered, ponderous gray underbellies close to the earth. The scent of rain was in the air. It seemed fitting.

Ellie made a call to Mr. Dalworthy, then bathed and found another of Rhiannon's outfits to wear; a dark suit, perfect for what she had to do. She met briefly with the farm manager, climbed into her car and headed toward London.

It started to rain on the outskirts of the city. Ellie flicked on the windshield wipers. The glass cleared, but her vision was still blurry. An instant later, the tears overflowed and stained her cheeks.

Parked outside Mr. Dalworthy's office, Ellie took a handkerchief from her purse, blew her nose and wiped her eyes. Getting out of the car she locked the door and entered the building.

"Elliana." The attorney rose and came around his desk when Ellie appeared in his doorway. He took her hand. "It's good to see you. How have you been faring?"

"Very well, thank you," she replied in an undertone.

Mr. Dalworthy frowned. "You look as though you've been crying. Are you really all right, Elliana? Are you sure you want to do this?"

"Oh, yes. Yes. I've never been more certain of anything."

The attorney nodded. "Come. Sit down then. I've mountains of papers for you to sign."

The paperwork took the majority of the afternoon. There were documents regarding her sister's estate as well as her divorce. Ellie wanted to get it all over with at once.

Ellie dotted the last 'i' over her name as thunder rumbled somewhere in the distance. "There. I guess that's it."

"I'm sorry to keep you so long, but..."

"No, this is fine. What do I have to do next?"

"Well, that will depend on George, of course," the attorney responded. "The settlement you've offered is generous. To a fault, I might add. If he's smart, he'll..."

Ellie laughed.

"Yes. I see what you mean." Mr. Dalworthy rubbed his chin. "Nevertheless, his own counsel will undoubtedly urge him to accept your terms. Then you will be a free woman."

"Mr. Dalworthy," Ellie said as she rose. "I'm a free woman already."

*   *   *

There was one last thing to do.

Mr. Dalworthy had informed her George had moved out of their flat and in with his mother. Ellie drove to their old apartment and let herself in.

He had left it as she had expected he would. She tripped over a dirty t-shirt on the way into the bedroom.

The only things left in the closet and bureau were hers. Ellie pulled out her bags and began packing. Once, she stopped and wondered why she bothered. But she would not, she told herself, be able to spend all her time with Valdemar. He had duties, as he had told her, and she had hers. The breeding program her sister had started had to continue. Ellie's work was cut out for her. She'd need to be dressed for it. Ellie clicked the last bag closed. Then she changed into the outfit she had chosen for her return to Valdemar; a shirt and sweater covered in hearts. Perfect. Dressed, she sat on the edge of the unmade bed. She picked up the phone.

George's mother answered.

"Just a moment," she sniffed. "I'll get him."

Ellie heard receding footsteps. Then a solid clumping, drawing nearer.

"Hullo?"

"Hello, George."

"What the bloody hell do *you* want?"

"I just wanted to say that I'm...I'm sorry, George. Sorry for everything. It was all just a big mistake."

"You're bloody telling *me*? Well, you can bugger off..."

"That's right, George. That's exactly what I'm doing. Buggering off. Goodbye."

Ellie hung up the phone. She picked up her bags, carried them down to the car and put them in the trunk.

A crack of thunder sounded directly overhead. The skies opened and the rain came down in earnest. Ellie closed her eyes, held out her arms and lifted her face.

In minutes she was soaked. Water ran from her in rivulets. Her wet hair was plastered to her back and shoulders. She smiled.

She was cleansed.

It was over.

*   *   *

The horse beneath her was surprisingly swift. Before, she and Valdemar had galloped in a leisurely fashion to the misty mountain. There had been no hurry, no urgency. Ellie had never known, until now, just what the animal was able to do. She clung to his mane, legs locked around his stout middle, as they raced across the plain.

Her heart was in her mouth. She couldn't help it. Why hadn't Valdemar been there to greet her?

"He awaits! He awaits!" Tiko had chirped.

"Where. *Where* does he 'await'?"

"He said only that," Fara opined.

"Yes," Tiko had chorused. "Only that."

There was only one place it could be. She hoped.

Ellie's mount scrambled up and over the foothills. The mist clung to her in a welcoming embrace. The hidden valley was revealed.

"Valdemar?"

There was no sign of him. Ellie urged her mount down into the valley. She slid from his back and ran to the edge of the pool. The mist began to swirl and eddy. A breeze sprang up. The mist gathered, began to take shape. Ellie turned and ran up the hill to the grand old willow.

He awaited her there, as Tiko had said. Hands on his hips, a smile on his lips. His chest was bare, the rest of him elegant and tantalizing in tight blue leggings.

"Valdemar," Ellie breathed.

"My queen."

She closed the space between them. He took her face in his hands and gently kissed her lips. "I love you," he murmured against her mouth. "For all time."

"As I love you. For all time." Ellie's lips parted in surrender. She pressed her body to Valdemar's. Twin whinnies shattered the silence.

Reluctantly, Ellie pulled away from her king. She turned in time to see the Spirit Horses galloping up the hill. They came to a sliding halt directly in front of the elven king and his queen. The stallion tossed his head, then reared and pawed at the sky. The mare walked quietly up to Ellie and nuzzled her belly.

"Can you hear what she's saying?" Valdemar asked quietly.

Ellie was still for a moment, listening. Her eyes filled with tears. They welled over and spilled down her cheeks.

"She's...she's in foal," Ellie whispered. A sob caught in her throat. She grasped

Valdemar's hand. "And so am I…"

Her vision blurred over completely. She heard the
horses whinny a parting tribute, and race away down the
hill. She turned back to Valdemar. A joy as boundless as
eternity flooded her soul. A playful smile danced on her
mouth.

"What, uh…what are you doing?" Valdemar asked,
watching his queen as she pulled her shirt up over her
head.

"Have you ever heard of a human game called
'Checkers'?" Ellie stepped out of her jeans and tossed them
aside.

"Um, no."

Ellie shrugged. She lay down on the grass,
squirmed a little to get comfortable, and lifted her arms to
Valdemar.

"So, what do you want me to do?" he inquired,
playing along.

Ellie grinned, "Just…'king me'…"

Helen A. Rosburg

And in ending,
let us begin
again.

~ H.R.